D1281361

Robin
and the
Silver Arrow

Tales of Robin Hood

This edition first published in 2009
by Sea-to-Sea Publications
Distributed by Black Rabbit Books
P.O. Box 3263
Mankato, Minnesota 56002

Text © Damian Harvey 2006, 2009
Illustration © Martin Remphry 2006

Printed in China

A CIP catalog record for this book is
available from the Library of Congress.

ISBN 978-1-59771-180-7

9 8 7 6 5 4 3 2 1

Published by arrangement with the
Watts Publishing Group Ltd, London.

Series Editor: Jackie Hamley
Series Advisors: Dr. Linda Gambrell, Dr. Barrie Wade
Series Designer: Peter Scoulding

HOPSCOTCH ADVENTURES

Robin
and the
Silver Arrow

by Damian Harvey and Martin Remphry

SEA-TO-SEA

Mankato Collingwood London

The Sheriff of Nottingham
was very pleased. He'd thought
of a way to catch Robin Hood.

The Sheriff had decided to hold an archery tournament. He was sure Robin would want to prove he was the best archer in the country.

Grand Archery
Tournament

The winner to
receive a
Silver Arrow
by order of the
Sheriff of
Nottingham.

And when he did, the Sheriff

would catch him!

News of the tournament soon
reached Sherwood Forest.
"The winner gets a silver arrow,"
said Much.

"I'll win that arrow," said Robin.

"No!" cried Will Scarlet,

"I'm sure it's a trap."

But Little John had an idea.

9

"Let's go in disguise," said Little
John. "Robin can wear gold, Will
can wear pink, and I'll go in blue.
No one will recognize us."

"Yes," laughed Robin. "And when
we get there, we can borrow the
Sheriff's soldiers' uniforms. He won't
be looking out for his own soldiers!"

The day of the tournament arrived
and crowds of people came.
Robin's merry men soon found
some uniforms to borrow.

The Sheriff and his soldiers kept
on the lookout for Robin Hood.
"He must be here!" said the Sheriff.

The archers lined up and took their first shots. Thud! Thud! Thud!

Many arrows hit their targets and the crowd cheered. Anyone who missed was out of the tournament.

The targets were moved further back and the archers fired again.

Thud! Thud! Thud!

Soon, only Robin Hood and one
of the Sheriff's soldiers were left.

The soldier fired and his arrow landed near the center of the target.

Then Robin fired.

Thud! His arrow landed right
in the center.

The soldier's second shot landed
right next to Robin's arrow.
Robin took careful aim and
fired his last arrow.

Thwak! Robin split the soldier's arrow in two. A huge cheer came up from the crowd. Robin had won!

"Ah ha!" said the Sheriff as he handed over the silver arrow. "There's only one person in England who can shoot like that ... Robin Hood. Arrest him!"

23

There was no escape for Robin.

The soldiers grabbed him.

"Not so fast," cried Little John.
"Let Robin go or you'll need to
find yourselves a new sheriff."

25

Robin and his merry men escaped back to Sherwood Forest and took the Sheriff with them.

If the soldiers came too close, one of Will's arrows sent them running.

Robin thanked the Sheriff for helping them escape, then sent him back to Nottingham ...

28

... but only after Little John had
taken his jewels!

"I don't think the Sheriff will ever forget the name of the best archer in England," laughed Little John. "It's Robin Hood!"

If you enjoyed this story, why not try another one?

There are 12 Hopscotch Adventures to choose from:

TALES OF KING ARTHUR

1. The Sword in the Stone
ISBN 978-1-59771-176-0

2. Arthur the King
ISBN 978-1-59771-173-9

3. The Round Table
ISBN 978-1-59771-175-3

4. Sir Lancelot and the Ice Castle
ISBN 978-1-59771-174-6

TALES OF ROBIN HOOD

Robin and the Knight
ISBN 978-1-59771-178-4

Robin and the Monk
ISBN 978-1-59771-179-1

Robin and the Friar
ISBN 978-1-59771-177-7

Robin and the Silver Arrow
ISBN 978-1-59771-180-7

MORE ADVENTURES

Aladdin and the Lamp
ISBN 978-1-59771-181-4

Blackbeard the Pirate
ISBN 978-1-59771-182-1

George and the Dragon
ISBN 978-1-59771-183-8

Jack the Giant-Killer
ISBN 978-1-59771-184-5